Petunia
and the
White Witch

By
Glenys Terry
and
Martin Howarth-Hynes snr

Published by Glenys Terry and Martin Howarth-Hynes snr

Publishing partner: Paragon Publishing, Rothersthorpe

ISBN 978-1-78222-967-4

Book design, layout and production management
by Into Print www.intoprint.net
01604 832149

Contents

Dedicated to our mum

Petunia

Petunia

I am a pensioner. My name is Petunia. I live on my own in a lovely cottage in a lovely village on Top Tipping street. The people in the village are kind and helpful.

My house has a garden. I love my garden and look after it all year round.

It makes me happy. People stop and chat and we share ideas and sometimes a cup of tea and slice of cake.

I have lived here, in this house, for a long time.

It was my auntie's house, my mum's sister.

I was always at my auntie's house. My auntie was a good woman and knew I wasn't happy at home.

Mum and dad hadn't wanted any children. So, when I came along I suspect I was a huge unwanted surprise.

In the end they decided to make the most of a *bad thing*.

As I grew up they made it abundantly clear that *I* was the bad thing. Everything I did was, in their eyes, wrong, not good enough and the harder I tried the more it hurt and the longer I cried.

I wasn't taken anywhere; to the park, to the cinema or even on holidays. Oh, I had everything I needed, nice clothes, toys, proper meals but no love, no kind words. I was just a burden, something they had to put up with.

I was alone and wondered what I had done to make them dislike me so much.

I did have an escape. When my parents wanted to go out or when they went on holidays, they took me to stay at my auntie's. My auntie was their opposite. She was kind and loving. She helped me with everything, we made cakes, painted, read books, told jokes. She took me to parks, the cinema and we sometimes went on short holidays to the seaside. I loved being with my auntie. She was to me the mum I always craved for.

The best thing was to help my auntie in her garden. We had so much fun, we planted many different kinds of flowers but mainly roses. There was one area which was special and only big red poppies grew there. This was in memory of my uncle. He died young, a hero in the second world war, that's why my auntie lived alone, she didn't want to marry again and hadn't any children. I suppose I compensated for that. Anyway, after our hard work in the garden we would sit for a while and chat; my auntie with her cup of tea and me with a glass of lemonade and of course, a slice of my auntie's homemade cake.

My auntie, unlike my parents, was very supportive through my school years and even helped me find my first job.

When my auntie passed away, she left me her house and that's where I am now ... and it's where I intend to stay.

The Naughty Children

The Naughty Children

Lately, a family has moved in down the road on Slip Drive. They have two children, a boy aged about nine years old and a girl a little older. They are very naughty!

They come into my garden and they **JUMP** and **SHOUT** and **STAMP** on my beautiful flowers and they are very cheeky to me.

I tell them to... *"Get out of my garden!"* and *"I know where you live!"* and *"I know your mum and dad!"* But they just run off laughing and calling me *rude* names and sticking their tongues out.

I just want a quiet life, peace and quiet, that's all. I feel so sad.

I invited my friend Tizzie Pops around for a cup of tea and a natter. When she arrived I told her about the naughty children and about what they say and what they do. She said she'd give them a clip round the ear or a kick up the bum. I thought, I'd like to see her do that, she is only five foot tall and has arthritis!

We then remembered Sheila the white witch who lived in Lower Naps Nest Lane just down the road. I decided to go and see her in the morning, to see if she could help. After all, she did help stop old Mrs Brown from spitting in the butchers shop *and* she got rid of Mr Robinson's loud and sudden eruptions of flatulence (which was a relief for all the village)! She just might have something to stop the naughty children too.

The White Witch

16

The White Witch

Morning arrived and I was up and ready for my visit to the white witch. I put on my raincoat because the weather had suddenly turned very cloudy and dark. The weather forecast said it was going to be sunny. Well, they were wrong.

I turned the corner that led to Lower Naps Nest Lane and there was Sheila's cottage. It was set apart from the other more modern houses and looked rather out of place. It was the sort of cottage that you would expect to see on a box of chocolates. I moved quickly up the pebbled path to the front door. The nearer I got the gloomier the sky became. At last I reached the front door and was about to ring the bell when the door suddenly slowly started to open, making a loud creaking noise as it did. A figure stood in the doorway, it was Sheila.

Sheila just stood there, staring at me.

Now, you would expect a white witch to

look beautiful, with long flowing white hair, blue eyes and a clear complexion. Sheila was pretty ugly! She looked like a witch that you see in story books. She had a big pointed nose, goodness it was **_HUGE_** and it had a wart on it, like a rock balancing on the end of a mighty cliff. Her hair was grey, long and scraggly and her chin had a few hairs protruding from the yellowish tinged skin. However, she did have the most beautiful, brightest, blue eyes I've ever seen.

"What do you want?" she said at last, with a rather gritty voice.

She stared right through me with those piercing blue eyes and I felt that she knew everything about me. I escaped from her stare and told her that I was here about the naughty children.

"*Mmmmmm*," she grunted. "You had better come in then."

She showed me into her sitting room, which was rather cluttered, there were books everywhere. Sheila waved her hand towards a chair for me to sit in and she sat facing me. Between us was a small table with two cups, two saucers and a teapot with steam coming out of the spout. So, she *was* expecting me. We sat staring at each other in silence. Then Sheila leaned forward and set her eyes on me. "Tell me!" she commanded.

I heard her voice echoing in my ears and I began to speak and found that I could not stop.

"It's those naughty kids, they keep coming into my garden and trampling on my flowers and calling me names, they throw things at me and at my door. All I want is to be left alone, I've tried to ignore them but then I end up shouting at them, shouting and shouting till my throat is sore…

"ENOUGH!" sputtered Sheila, her eyes bulging and her mouth slavering. She banged her bony fist on the table making the crockery clatter loudly. "I've heard enough of your blimmin yatting, you're making my ears bleed!"

That's a bit rude I thought. Sheila stared into my eyes once more, those blue eyes were so mesmerizing. She spoke again, this time her voice was softer but still with the hint of witch.

"What do you want me to do about it dear?" she poured herself a cup of tea.

"Well you're a white witch," I said. "Can't you make those kids behave?"

"Have a cup of tea my dear, it's green tea, it's good for you."

Before I could answer she had the tea poured and was handing it to me.

I took a sip. *Ugh* it was horrible! It made me wince and splutter. I could feel Sheila's eyes on me again.

"Everything alright?" she asked. And I'm sure she was smirking. Those eyes now had a playful glint in them.

"Oh yes, thank you... it's very... *different.*"

Oh it was disgusting! But I could not help looking at her nose. Every time she took a drink her nose with the wart disappeared into her cup and dipped into the horrible green liquid. And when she lifted it up there was a green droplet balancing on the very tip and threatening to drip with a plop at any moment.

I felt a giggle coming up from my stomach, I tried to stop it by taking a mouthful of the green tea, but then Sheila's cat walked in. It looked like a ball of black wool, like it had had an electric shock. Sheila picked it up and began to cuddle it.

"Ooooh my little cuddly wuddly kitty witty poohs, does kitty witty want to sit on mumsy wumsies knee then? Oooh yes she does, ooh yes she does."

Well, I tried to keep my giggle from exploding up from my tummy, but I could not stop it any longer and my tea spurted out of my mouth with a *whoooooooooosh...*

… all over Sheila and her cat!

My giggle had escaped and for a moment I could not stop it!

What did stop it was the fact that Sheila and her cat were both glaring at me, the green tea dripping from their faces.

"Something funny?" asked Sheila, as she wiped the horrid green liquid from her face. The cat hissed at me with contempt. That cat did *not* like me.

"How dare you," croaked Sheila, her eyes popping out of her head. "How dare you spit tea on me and my poor kitty witty!"

I told Sheila that I was really sorry and that the lovely tea had gone down the wrong way and made me choke. I had lied. Well, I couldn't tell her that I was laughing at her big hooter could I?

"Mmmmmm," she grunted. Then she got out of her chair, picked her cat up by the scruff of its neck and kicked it out of the back door. Now, I don't condone kicking any animal, but I was glad it was gone, that cat gave me the creeps.

"Right, began Sheila, let's get down to business."

She sat facing me once more, then poked her thin bony finger up her nose and pulled out some snot, but what really turned my stomach was that she then thrust the gooey bogey into her mouth. When she had chewed it enough she took a swig of her foul tea. I didn't think I could take any more of her filth. Then she let out a loud *trump!* "Ahhhh," she croaked, "that's better." She caught my gaze once more. "Have you tried to ignore these children?"

I told Sheila that I had tried and tried, but it was no use. They start shouting and calling me rude names like; Mrs wobbly bottom or wrinkly old woman.

"Mmmmmm," grunted Sheila.

"Have you tried throwing stones at them?"

"No, I said. I wouldn't want to hurt them, anyway they would just throw them back and smash my windows or they might call the police."

"Mmmmmm," grunted Sheila. "Pity. Have you told their parents?"

"Yes, I said. But all they do is shout at me. Once, one parent said a naughty word then slammed the door in my face."

"What was the naughty word?" asked Sheila, more interested now.

"I don't like to say."

"Was it @##** ~'!!*?" asked Sheila.

"Yes," I said quickly and my face began to

feel very hot.

"Mmmmmm," grunted Sheila. "I see."

Sheila thought for a moment. She tapped her bony chin with a bony long finger. Then, with a sudden movement she jumped out of her chair and grabbed a dusty old book from her bookcase. It was a book of spells.

It said on the cover: *THE GOOD WHITE WITCH'S GUIDE TO GOOD SPELLS.*

"Now let me see." croaked Sheila as she slammed the big heavy book on the table, sending a cloud of dust rising up to the ceiling. She then licked her long bony thumb with her almost purple tongue making a loud *SLURPING* noise and began to turn the pages. Each page that she turned she would lick her thumb.

SLURP, SLURP, SLURP!

"Mmmmmm, yes," she suddenly croaked exitedly, then just as quickly: "Mmmmmm, no that won't do at all." Another page, another thumb lick, "Mmmmmm no no no. Maybe, no." Then...

She slammed her wrinkly hand on top of the page.

"This is the one!" she announced. A strand of spittle flew from her mouth and her eyes bulged wildly. In her joy she began to do a little

dance and to punch the air with her fist. "Eat my bloomers naughty children!" she screeched. She began to cackle and mumble to herself, I think it was more naughty words.

"Have you found something?" I asked at last.

"Yes of course I have…erm…erm, what did you say your name was dear?"

I said that I hadn't told her my name.

"Well, what is it then?" spluttered the weary white witch.

"Petunia," I said.

"Petunia!" she repeated. "What a bleedin stupid name that is." Then she began to cackle even more.

I thought, well, that's a bit rude.

Suddenly there was a bright flash of lightning and a loud rumble of thunder which made Sheila cackle excitedly. She returned to the opened page in the spell book.

"Mmmmmm…" she croaked. "What we need is:

A bat's toenail
A slimy snail
A little bit of this
A little bit of that
Some fur from a cat
And that will be that!"

I asked Sheila if there was such a thing as a bat's toenail. She answered very impatiently as if I had asked the stupidest question ever.

"Of course there blimmin is! Otherwise it wouldn't be in this book would it?" She emphasized each word and spat it out as if it had created a bad taste in her mouth. Although, I thought, there were enough bad tastes already in her mouth, considering the stench of her breath.

"And what is more," she began, "I have all these things in my collection of spell conjuring ingredients, especially *BAT'S TOENAILS!*"

She searched my face for a reaction, and I was about to say that I have not seen any evidence of a collection of any sort, only books. But, before I could open my mouth, she leaped over to her bookcase and with a wide witchy smirk said; "What about this then?" Sheila gave the cupboard a twack with her booted foot and stood facing me with that wide somewhat smug smile.

I think something should have happened, Sheila once again was waiting for my reaction. All I could do was shrug my shoulders questioningly.

Sheila turned around to see that what should have happened hadn't.

"Mmmmmm," she grunted. Then she said another naughty word and gave the cupboard a hefty kick. Suddenly things started to change. The shelves with the books on spun around, then the books disappeared in a haze of dust and in their place appeared hundreds of phials, jars and bottles. Each one contained a witchy ingredient for a specific magic spell. My eyes wandered around the mass of spells and there, almost hidden behind another phial of gunge, was a jar with a label. The label read: BAT'S TOENAILS.

I was astounded!

"I bet you're astounded aren't you?" beamed Sheila, knowingly.

I told her that what I had just witnessed was absolutely amazing.

"Well, it's not one of my better spells, she mused, but it keeps those things hidden and out of sight from those pesky nosey gits from the village."

Sheila then reached for the bat's toenail jar and moved toward her gas fire. She tapped the fire and the whole thing whirled around so fast it became a blur. When it had stopped it was no longer a modern gas fire but a large open fireplace. And suspended over the crackling logs was a large round cauldron.

The cauldron bubbled with a green liquid. Sheila took a bat's toenail slowly out of the jar, she mumbled a few words then dropped it in the hot green gluppy stuff.

Immediately, there was a puff of smoke and the whole cauldron spat and hissed. Sheila cackled then moved back to the phials, jars and bottles.

"Mmmmmm," she grunted. "Now for the slimy snail." She found the bottle with the slimy snail almost immediately. Then, she moved back to the cauldron. As before she took the slimy snail slowly out of the bottle, spoke a few witchy words then dropped it into the cauldron. It hissed and spat and crackled. "Mmmmmm," grunted Sheila. "Now for a bit of this." She dropped something into the cauldron,what it was we will never know. She did the same with a little bit of that. Both times the cauldron hissed,crackled and spat. "Mmmmmm," grunted Sheila. "Now for the last ingredient."

Sheila moved quickly to her back door and went outside. For a moment there was silence then... a loud squeal and a hiss. Sheila came back into the room clutching a bony handful of fur.

It was her cat's fur.

"Don't worry, '' she said at last, noticing my

concern. "It will grow back."

She then whispered some more strange mystical words, then dropped the fur into the cauldron. The cauldron hissed, crackled and spat, this time *higher and louder, higher and louder, higher and louder and louder and LOUDER!* Until at last, with a huge ***BANG!*** ... the potion was ready!

Immediately the fireplace, the cupboard, the phials, the bottles and the jars physled away and the room returned to as it was when I arrived.

Sheila held the potion aloft. "Here it is my dear," she said proudly. She then placed it in the palm of my hand. And slowly, with deliberation, folded my fingers around it. She set her big eyes on me again. "When those children come to your house," she began, in a low croaky whisper. "It will be time to drink the potion."

I was dumb struck for a moment, I still had my doubts. Then, I asked a question which I really wish I hadn't.

"Will it work?"

"You're asking me if the potion will work?"

"Yes."

"You're *really* asking *me* if the potion will work?"

"Yes."

"So, let's get this straight, *YOU* are asking *ME* if the *POTION* will really work?"

"Yes."

Sheila put her face close up to mine and started to speak in a slow menacing voice.

"You're asking me, Sheila, a wise white witch, what knows a white witching spell that will work well when I see one, if the potion which I have conjured from a white witch spell book, that has been used successfully for centuries ... *IF... IT... WILL ... WORK?!*"

"Yes."

"Mmmmmm," she croaked angrily, *"OF COURSE IT WILL WORK!!!!!"* Sheila's eyes were now wide and wild. She spat every word out so loudly that the room seemed to shake.

Touched a nerve there, I thought.

Then, I quickly thanked Sheila for the potion. I had a feeling it was time to go.

"You'll be going now will you, my dear?" she asked with a menacing frown.

I was right, it *was* time to go.

She then put her face even closer, so close that I could smell her foul breath, it made me feel quite queasy.

"Don't worry my dear, you'll soon be rid of those naughty children. Then in a low almost whisper, "Hold tight to the phial with the potion, there are dark forces that would steal it from your grasp and use it for their own evil mischief."

Before I could answer she took me by the arm and showed me to her door.

She opened the door and her cat ran in from the storm. As it passed me, it gave me a scowling glance and hissed. A large bald patch could be seen quite clearly in the middle of its arched back.

Sheila sniffed, then wiped her nose on her already matted sleeve.

"Goodbye and good luck," she said, then pushed me out of her doorway into the street and slammed the door quickly behind her. Immediately there was a flash of lightning and a rumble of thunder. The weather had gotten worse. The wind was so strong it was hard to walk. Leaves were blowing off the trees and doing a strange dance in front of me. Round and round they went. A man ran past me chasing his hat that had blown off revealing his shiny bald head.

Lightning flashed, thunder roared, trees were swaying, their branches seemed like spindly, bony grasping hands that clowed the air as I passed them... And now it had begun to rain!

I leant against the wind and rain and forced my way home. With each step The storm became worse. It was as though someone or something was holding me back with some sort of mystical force.

At last I reached my door, I fumbled in my pocket for my key. Instead I pulled out the potion and as I did I felt that same force trying to prise my hand open. Somehow I kept my grip. I found my key and tried to put it in my lock, again that same force was pushing my hand away. Three times I tried to put the key in the lock, the fourth attempt I mustered all my strength and thrust the key into the lock and turned it with a click. At that very moment the storm was gone. All was calm and the sun started to appear from the diminishing clouds.

I stepped in my house, glad to be home.

"*Phew*, that was a bit dramatic," I thought. I then quickly checked my pocket for the potion. It was still there. I needed a nice cup of tea, not like Sheila's, that was horrible, the thought of it made me feel quite ill.

So, I made a cup of tea, switched my gas fire on, as the room had gotten quite chilly. I then flopped into my comfy chair. "That's better," I sighed. I put the potion next to my tea cup and got to thinking...

What would happen if I tried just a little, tiny, itsy, bitsy sip of the potion?

Surely a little taste wouldn't do any harm.

The Monster

The Monster

SO, I HAD A LITTLE DRINK!
UGH!

It was *slimy!* It was *phooey!* It was *chewy!* and it was... rather nice really, in a strange mad sort of way.

I then waited for something to happen.

I didn't feel any different.

Then, I began to think that Sheila might be a bit mad, and that I was even madder to have believed her.

"Knickers!" I said out loud, in frustration and I was about to fling the phial of potion across the room. But as I reached out my hand the telephone began to ring. I got out of my comfy seat, still a bit disgruntled, and picked up the receiver.

"Hello," I said.

"Hello Petunia, it's me Sheila, I'm just calling

to say I forgot to tell you about an after effect the potion may have."

"Oh yes," I answered, expecting more of her witchy madness.

"Yes, after you have taken a sip of the potion you will have a bit of erm... uncontrollable flatulence...It will be quite loud, have you taken any of the potion?"

Before I could answer I let out an enormous *trump!* It was so loud I thought that someone walking past my house would hear. I felt very embarrassed. I heard Sheila cackle on the other end of the phone.

"I'll take that as a yes then." And with a click, she hung up.

Before I could process what had just happened, there was a loud knock at my door. "Who the blimmin ecks that!" I was quite annoyed now, having been disturbed twice from my cosy chair and cup of tea. I bounded to the door and swung it open, to be met by a young woman dressed rather smartly; black skirt, white blouse, black matching jacket and on the jacket was pinned a white rosett. The lady was looking down at a clip board with a few names on.

"I wonder," she began, "if we could count on your support in the local elections?" Then, she looked up from her clipboard and the smile that she had on her face a moment ago disappeared. Instead, on her face was an expression of total horror. She looked at me, her mouth wide open and silent. Then, she let out an enormous scream.

"WHAAAAAAAAAAAAAAAAAAA!"

I let out an enormous scream.

"WHAAAAAAAAAAAAAAAAAAA!"

The young lady then threw her arms in the air, quickly turned and ran screaming down my path and into the street.

"She's bloomin' mad," I said to myself, then I went back into my house slamming the door angrily behind me with a loud thud and ...
a very loud trump!

I stomped through my hallway. And as I did, I happened to glance in the mirror that hung there.

"WHAAAAAAAAAAAAAA!"

From my passing glance I thought I saw the most hideous of faces glaring back at me, so I threw myself out of its vision and fell to the floor. I stayed there for a few moments quietly convincing myself that it was just my imagination, for there was no room facing the mirror, there was only me in the hallway.

ONLY ME IN THE HALLWAY!

I was panicking again. But eventually I mustered enough courage to slowly get to my feet and then, with great caution, I peered into the mirror. There, staring back at me was the hideous face that I had seen a moment ago. I wanted to scream again but instead I put a hand to my mouth to stop me. At that very same time the ...thing...put its hand to its mouth.

I put my hand down,it put its hand down. I raised my other hand, it raised it's other hand. Then, I realised that the hideous monster *must be me!*

The monster was covered it black fur which was stuck up like it had had an electric shock. Rather like Sheila's cat. Its eyes were red, its teeth were long and green, and its nose was wide with nostrils like a bulls. Its hands were huge like a bears and it had claws for fingernails. Long, sharp, black claws! It had short muscular legs and its feet were like its hands huge like a bears and those same long, sharp black, claws. But then I noticed something quite peculiar. When I looked in the mirror *I* was the monster. When I looked at myself away from the mirror I saw only *me*. Me as the world and I see me. No wonder I didn't notice anything earlier.

So, when I take the potion, everyone sees the monster, except me, unless I look in a mirror. *"Bonkers!"* I thought to myself. But if it gets rid of those naughty children like it did that lady a moment ago *YIPPPPPPEEEEEEE!*

And to make everything even clearer I did another very *LOUD THUNDEROUS TRUMP!*

I felt tired after that. So, after putting the potion in a safe place, I dragged myself to bed and fell into a well deserved, deep slumber.

ॐ

When I at last awoke, I felt quite invigorated. Although, there was a nasty taste in my mouth, which I put down to the potion.

It was a beautiful day; the sun was bright, the little birds were singing happily in the trees . The scent from my rose garden blew in from the open window of my bedroom. And, I couldn't wait to get out there.

I jumped out of bed and got myself washed and dressed. The mirror in the bathroom which I had glanced in with a little trepidation, only reflected my image, not the monster's, so that was ok.

I had my breakfast with a nice cup of tea. Then I went out into my lovely garden taking the potion with me. If those naughty children come here today, I would be ready for them!

I didn't have to wait long.

As I was giving one of my pot plants a little water, I heard giggling from behind one of the bushes that borders my garden. And beyond that is a public path. The naughty children were back! Then a stone hit my watering can with a loud PING! I warned them to go away and behave or they would be sorry. But all I got was abuse.

"OH WHAT YOU GOING TO DO MISS WOBBLY BOTTOM!" The girl shouted, and the giggles got louder.

"Yeah," added the boy. "What you going to do Miss stinky wobbly bottom!" Then they started to chant. *"Wobbly bottom, wobbly bottom, big, big, wobbly, wobbly bottom!"*

Oh, they thought they were so funny and clever. And I was getting angry, so when they jumped into my garden and started to kick the heads off my flowers, I could not take any more. *"RIGHT YOU'RE FOR IT NOW!"* I shouted. Of course they ignored me. Oooooooh I was really angry, so I reached for the potion which was in my pocket, popped the lid off and took a big *gulp!*

And waited...

This time I could feel something happening, I glanced over towards one of the windows of my house so that I could see in the reflection if I had changed.

Yes I had. So, I let out a growl, an angry growl, a deep, thundering growl so terrifying that it even frightened me. I had gotten the naughty children's attention. The look of terror on their faces was very satisfying. I then leaped over a pot plant towards the children and growled again, this time even louder – and to add to that, I let out a *MIGHTY TRUMP*.

The naughty children *SCREAMED!* They were bumping into each other trying to get away.

"GO!" I shouted with my big deep growly voice. *"GO ... **NOW!**"*

The naughty children pushed through one of the bushes like a pair of scurrying rats. They got onto the path and ran towards their home, screaming all the way.

When they were gone and out of sight I quickly went indoors, just in case someone else might happen to see me. I was beginning to feel quite exhausted. All that growling and trumping takes it out of a little old lady like me. I bounded into my sitting room and flopped into my comfy armchair and waited for the potion to wear off.

Barbara

Barbara

It must have been only fifteen minutes later, when I was awoken abruptly by loud knocking at my door. I was getting a bit fed up with people knocking at my door when I was having a nice rest. Anyway, I sleepily got out of my chair and went reluctantly to see who the over zealous visitor was. I glanced in the mirror as I passed, just to check if I was still monsterfied. To my relief, I wasn't.

I reached the door.

"Who is it?"

"Just open the blimmin door, you old bat!" came the loud and rather rude response.

"Not until you tell me who you are." Although I had an idea it was the naughty children's mum.

"It's Sally and John's mum from down't street."

"Oh, the naughty children's mum?"

"Yes... er, what, no. Look, are you goin' to open the door or what?"

I opened the door slowly, to reveal on my doorstep; Mrs Tip from Slip street, the naughty children's mum. I was right, but wasn't happy about it.

"Can I help you my dear?" I was aware that I sounded a little like Sheila.

The naughty children's mum was quite well turned out, pretty, slim with neat dark hair that was held in place with a red Alice band. It was a pity that when she opened her mouth to speak, she sounded rough and quite common.

"My kids have just come 'ome, screamin' an' cryin', sayin' you set a monster on 'em!"

"Well, they were here earlier. I heard them in my garden then I saw them throwing stones. As soon as they saw me they started to call me rude names. Then, they just ran away laughing. As for me sending a monster after them, well, I don't believe in monsters, Mrs Trip, do *you*?"

"Yes... er, no... but summit scared them and they said it wer you!"

"Children have vivid imaginations, Mrs Trip. They were probably scared by Mr Peter's dog, it's big and has a very loud bark. Maybe it was that that scared the poor little mites."

"Well, I dunno... I suppose so, but..."

Before she could utter another word, I surprised her by asking to sit in my garden and have a nice cup of tea and a piece of cake, where we could chat about all this mix up.

"Well, I dunno, my Bert will be expecting me back and—"

"Oh, come on... erm... What's your first name?"

"Barbara."

"Very nice. Come on Barbara, I'll show you the way."

To my suprise Barbara followed me quietly into the garden.

"Oh, int it lovely," she gasped, "it's a beautiful garden innit?"

"Oh thank you. It's a lot of hard work but I enjoy it."

"Well, you've done yourself proud... erm..."

"Petunia."

"Yeah, you've done yourself right proud Petunia!"

I left Babara to explore my garden whilst I made a pot of tea. I also cut us a large slice of my homemade lemon cake. I brought the tea and cake to the garden and placed them on the wicker table. We then sat in the garden chairs. I poured the tea and offered Babara some cake.

"Oh ta," she said. Then she took a large bite.

"*Oooooooooh, mmmmmm*, did you mek this yerself?"

"Yes. Do you like it?"

"Do I *like* it, I should say I do, it's dead nice!"

"Thank you." I smiled to myself; yet another compliment from Barbara, who would have thought?

We chatted for a long time. Chatted and laughed, we were getting on really well.

"Do you like it 'ere Petunia?" Barbara asked.

"Oh, yes."

"You never married then?"

"No."

"Why not? There's a hubby out there missin' out of some right nice cake."

I didn't want to answer, but, for some inexplicable reason, I felt I had to.

"Well, you see, I always thought that I wasn't good enough. I was always bullied at school, I don't know why, I never did anyone any harm, I was always polite and good mannered... maybe that was it. Anyway, from then on I kept myself to myself. My mother said that I wouldn't amount to anything and that no sane man would want to marry me because I was so plain looking. So, I have been here alone all my life really. Oh, I have friends who come and see me and we go for lunch... but, I always wanted to marry a nice man, have children... maybe two, like you."

Barbara, who had listened to my ranting, quietly smiled. But, as hard as she wanted to appear, I could see the beginnings of a tear starting to emerge from the corner of her eye.

"It was not to be," I continued. "So here I am, Oh, don't get me wrong, I *am* happy, especially when I come out here... in my garden, it makes me happy and I can dream."

"Cobblers!" blurted out Barbara with a wry smile. "There must be someone who yer fancy, int there someone int village that yer like?"

Again Barbara surprised me with her question, and I just blurted my answer out.

"Well, yes... I suppose I like Mr Robinson... he's nice."

Babara laughed.

"What, old *farty pants Robinson!*"

"Well, yes... *no!*... He's not... he's cured... he's not inflicted with uncontrollable..."

"Farting?" smirked Barbara.

"Flatulence... not for a long time now and he's always kind to me. Once he helped me on the bus by carrying my shopping bag, when he handed it back he accidentally touched my hand. I went quite red, I'm sure he noticed."

"Ooooh, you little minx," laughed Babara.

Babara leant forward and in a lower voice than usual... she suggested that I invite him here for tea and cake.

"Oh, no, I couldn't!" I protested. Secretly I thought that it was a good idea.

"Why not? You asked me 'ere and you can't have liked me that much, and I can be a bit gobby too."

"A *bit*?"

"Oy, checky," she laughed. "But why not ask im, you might be pleasantly surprised."

"No... I—"

"That's settled then," interrupted Babara. "You can ask 'im tomorrow, he always buys a loaf from Susan's cake shop int village at 10 o'clock sharp, you can set your watch by im... be there, it could change your life!"

"But, what if he says no?"

"Well, at least you'll have asked. Anyway, never give up, that's what I always say."

I took a sip of my now tepid tea and mused over what Babara had just said.

"Very well... tomorrow at 10," I said at last.

"Great!" shouted Babara. "I've a feeling you won't regret it."

"So, what about you?"

"What do you mean?"

"Well, I've told you my dark secrets, what about you... have you had a good life, are you happy?"

Babara thought for a moment. Her smile that she had on her face a moment ago vanished and instead she began to look so sad, lost and vulnerable, not the Barbara I thought I now knew.

"I'm happy now..."

I could tell there was something in her past that was troubling her, I didn't press her, I waited, gave her time to collect her thoughts.

"I was told," she began, "that when I was five, me and me four sisters were taken into care...

Mum couldn't look after us, she was on her own you see. Dad was useless, always drunk and he left mum and us for another woman in Manchester.

Mum was so sad and alone. She tried to look after us but she lost her job, 'cuttin back' they said. So, she couldn't pay the rent... She just couldn't cope. Oh my poor mum, we must have driven her up the blimmin wall.

Eventually, she took to drinking. And that was that. Social services noticed summit was up cos of the way we were at school, when we were there; scruffy and hungry we were. So, they split us up.

I was five, Sally was seven, the twins Margret and Sarah were nine, and Ellen, the oldest, was eleven. We were all fostered out. I remember being told I was going on holiday and my sisters were too, but to a different place... I never saw or heard from them or my mum again..." Barbara's words trailed off into uncontrollable sobs.

"Oh, you poor thing," I said at last. "Have you tried to find your mum and sisters Barbara?"

"Yes, I did try a few years ago, before I had the kids. But it was difficult, I didn't know where to start and who to ask. I tried online too but no joy there. My foster parents only knew what I've told you. And I don't know where they are, we lost touch over the years.

So, I have no idea where they are. Every day I think about them, and wonder if they are thinkin' about me." Babara began to sob again. I vowed there and then, that I would do everything that I could, to help find her mum and siblings.

Barbara announced that she had to go.

"My Bert'll be chewin' at the bit, and I've been here long enough... and... you know summit Petunia... you're all right."

"So are you, Barbara." And as I said those words, I thought of the old saying 'Never judge a book by its cover.' After our chat over tea and cake, I certainly now saw Barbara in a different light.

We said goodbye and as Barbara got to the bottom of my path, she turned and smiled.

"Don't you forget tomorrow," she ordered, pointing a finger. "Mr. Robinson 10 o'clock sharp."

"I won't forget," I replied. And I felt butterflies flutter in my stomach at the very thought.

Mr Robinson

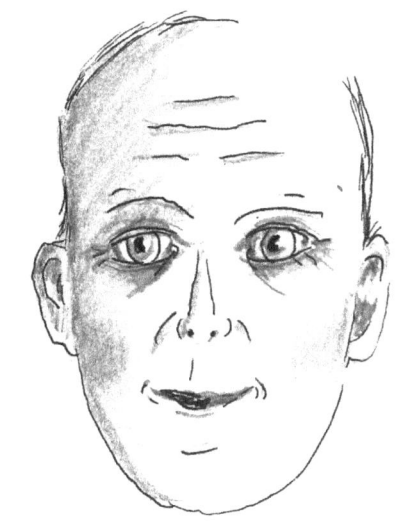

Mr Robinson

The next day, Susan's bakery shop, 10 o'clock. I was right on time... and so was Mr Robinson. After a lot of muddling my words, I finally asked Mr Robinson – or Tom as he said I should call him – to have tea and cake in my garden the following day. To my utter surprise, he agreed.

It was a wonderful day, everything went so well. It was as if I had known him all my life and Tom said that he felt the same.

Then, three months later and out of the blue, Tom proposed, and of course I said YES!

Soon after we had married, I told Tom about Barbara and her mum and sisters and how, or if, we could help. It turned out that Tom's brother was a whizz at family trees and finding lost relatives – a hobby of his. What a stroke of luck I thought, everything seems to be falling into place. And, after just five weeks of looking. Barbara's family was found... All of them!

And she has lots of nephews and nieces. Also, Barbara's mum is well and hasn't had a drink for years. She had thought, wrongly, that her daughters would not want to see her, so didn't look for them. The surprising thing is that they all live within a thirty mile radius. I couldn't wait to tell Barbara!

Barbara was unbelievably happy at the news. She looked different, radiant, bright and the years seemed to have fallen from her face.

Barbara planned to meet her mum and siblings in a few weeks time. I wished her all the luck in the world...

Visitors

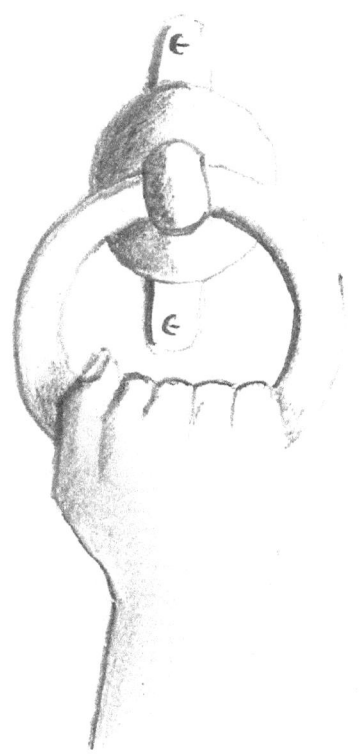

Visitors

One day, Tom and I were in the garden chatting over a cup of tea. The weather was good and we had been busy pruning the roses – we have a lot of roses – so, we thought we deserved a well earned rest.

We were halfway through our cups of tea, when suddenly there was a loud knock at the door. When I opened the door, I was surprised to see standing there, not only Barbara but her four sisters *and* her mum. Barbara wanted to introduce them to me and Tom. They had brought some cake to celebrate.

We all got on so well, it was a lovely surprise and we had a lovely day together.

When it was time to go, Barbara's mum came up to me and grabbed hold of my hand and with tears rolling down a face that had aged much quicker than it should have, she said in a whisper:

"Thank you... thank you Petunia."

Barbara pops round regularly and gives us updates on her mum and sisters. She shows us lots of photos of her new found nephews and nieces.

Barbara's children come round too. They help in the garden and sometimes we help them with their homework.

All this would have been unbelievable a few months ago. Everything has changed so much... for the better. I have a husband, lots of new friends and the naughty children are far from naughty. Now, they are so respectful.

A Passing Glance

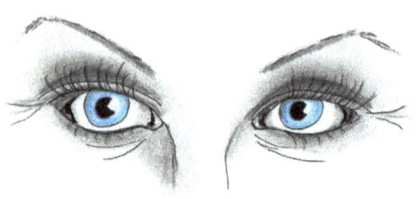

64

A Passing Glance

Yes, I am so happy now.

And, do you know, it's all down to Sheila the white witch. It is as though it was all part of her plan.

I never saw Sheila after my visit to her cottage. She's not there now and her cottage has been taken over by a young family.

However, there was a time, not long after Barbara's family's visit to my home, when I was at the village market looking for some tulip bulbs. I happened to glance across the road, and my eyes fell on a young lady, rather striking in appearance with a pale complexion, white flowing hair...

and... those eyes...bright, mesmerizing, bright blue eyes. The young woman seemed to sense my presence and looked towards me and smiled. Then, to my surprise, she lifted her hand slowly and waved. It was like it happened in slow motion like you would see in a film. I had the urge to wave back, but as I began to lift my hand in response, the village bus hurtled by blocking my view. And when it had gone... so had the young lady.

Could that have been Sheila?

I like to think that it was.

Final

Final

Back in my garden, I was thinking about Sheila and how she had changed so many lives. And the happiness that she had brought into those lives.

I gazed dreamily into the distance, just thinking, quietly thinking.

Then, out loud and with a smile, I said...

"Thank you Sheila."

And on the rose-scented breeze, I thought I heard a whispered reply...

"You're welcome, my dear."